AW YEAH COMICS!™

ACTION CAT™ & ADVENTURE BUG

AW YEAH COMICS!™

ACTION CAT™ & ADVENTURE BUG

STORY BY ART BALTAZAR AND FRANCO

ARTWORK BY ART BALTAZAR

DARK HORSE BOOKS

President and Publisher **MIKE RICHARDSON**
Editor **SHANTEL LaROCQUE**
Assistant Editor **KATII O'BRIEN**
Designer **SARAH TERRY**
Digital Art Technician **CHRISTINA McKENZIE**

Published by Dark Horse Books
A division of Dark Horse Comics, Inc.
10956 SE Main Street | Milwaukie, OR 97222

DarkHorse.com ★ AwYeahComics.com

First edition: October 2016
ISBN 978-1-50670-023-6

1 3 5 7 9 10 8 6 4 2
Printed in China

This volume collects *Aw Yeah Comics!: Action Cat & Adventure Bug* #1–#4, originally published by Dark Horse Comics.

AW YEAH COMICS!: ACTION CAT & ADVENTURE BUG

Library of Congress Cataloging-in-Publication Data

Names: Baltazar, Art, author, illustrator. | Aureliani, Franco, author, illustrator.
Title: Aw yeah comics! : Action Cat & Adventure Bug / story by Art Baltazar and Franco ; art by Art Baltazar.
Description: First edition. | Milwaukie, OR : Dark Horse Books, 2016. | "This volume collects Aw Yeah Comics!: Action Cat & Adventure Bug #1-#4, originally published by Dark Horse Comics." | Summary: The heroes, Action Cat and Adventure Bug, run a comics shop called Aw Yeah Comics, but Evil Cat, looking to do evil, lurks behind the scenes with his new secret weapon, the Lizard Gun.
Identifiers: LCCN 2016021903 | ISBN 9781506700236 (paperback)
Subjects: LCSH: Graphic novels. | CYAC: Graphic novels. | Superheroes--Fiction. | BISAC: JUVENILE FICTION / Comics & Graphic Novels / General.
Classification: LCC PZ7.7.B33 Au 2016 | DDC 741.5/973--dc23
LC record available at https://lccn.loc.gov/2016021903

CHAPTER ONE

AW YEAH DARK HORSE COMICS PROUDLY PRESENTS...

CORNELIUS! ALOWICIOUS!

AW YEAH HAMMOND!
HERE WE COME WITH THE MORNING COFFEE!

THANKS!
WE HAVE LOTS OF BACK ISSUES TO SORT!
LET'S GET TO WORK!

BAG!
BAG!

TAPE
TAPE

FILE
FILE

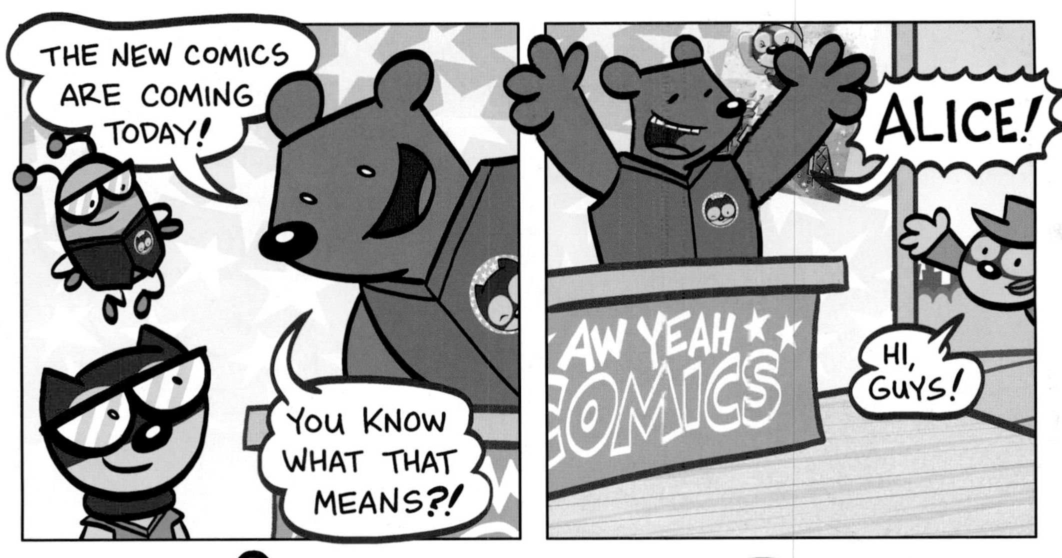
THE NEW COMICS ARE COMING TODAY!
YOU KNOW WHAT THAT MEANS?!
ALICE!
AW YEAH COMICS
HI, GUYS!

AW YEAH!
THE NEW COMICS ARE HERE!

DON'T ACT SO HAPPY TO SEE ME, CORNELIUS.
MAKE IT SNAPPY.
SIGN

OH, NO. IT'S EVIL CAT!
WHAT'S THAT EVIL FIEND DOING HERE?
I'M NOT SURE.

WELCOME TO AW YEAH COMICS!
MAY I HELP YOU, SIR?
WHERE'S ACTION CAT?!
I KNOW YOU GUYS KNOW WHERE HE IS!
AW YEA

I WANT TO TURN HIM INTO A LIZARD WITH MY LIZARD GUN!

WHY?
BECAUSE!
THAT'S WHY!

I DON'T HAVE TO EXPLAIN MYSELF TO YOU!
I'M EVIL CAT!

EXCUSE ME, EVIL CAT...
...WOULD YOU CARE TO STEP OUTSIDE?

WHO ARE YOU?
I'M ACTION CAT!
NO, YOU'RE NOT...
YES, I AM!

WELL... UM... NOT YOU THEN.
...PER SE...
I MEANT THE OTHER ONE.
THE BOY ONE.

OH, I SEE.
WELL, WHILE YOU MAKE UP YOUR MIND...

HEY!

...TRY COOLING OFF IN THIS COMIC BOOK LONG BOX!

CURSE YOU, ACTION CAT!
SEE? NOW YOU'RE GETTING IT.

WOW! ACTION CAT! YOU MADE IT!
GOOD JOB CAPTURING EVIL CAT!
HELLO, HAMMOND.
WE'RE HERE!

OH, HEY.
ALREADY TAKEN CARE OF.

THANKS, ADORABLE... AHEM!
ACTION CAT!
YES...
UM...
ACTION CAT...

...WE'LL TAKE IT FROM HERE.
SURE YOU WILL.

THE BAD GUY IS IN THIS BOX.
GGRRRR!

HEH,
HEH, HEH.
HAVE AT IT, BOYS!
GRAB

ZAP!
WATCH OUT!
THIS BOX CANNOT CONTAIN MY EVILNESS!
ZZP!
TAKE THAT, HEROES!
BZAP!
EMBRACE YOUR REPTILIAN FATE!

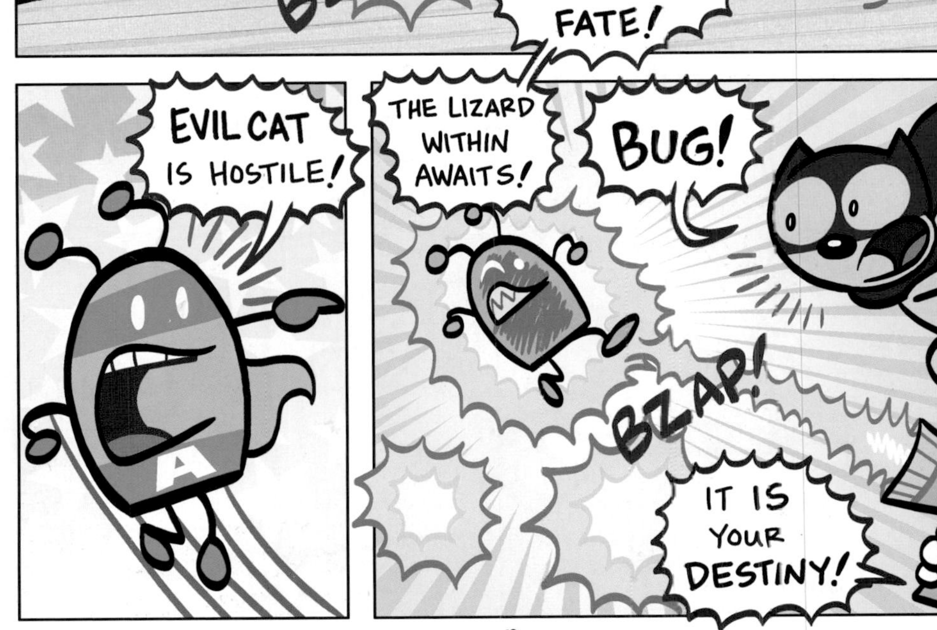
EVIL CAT IS HOSTILE!
THE LIZARD WITHIN AWAITS!
BUG!
BZAP!
IT IS YOUR DESTINY!

—TO BE CONTINUED...

SPOT VS. MARQUAID
YOU DON'T KNOW THE POWER OF THE CRYSTAL!
LOOKS LIKE A LITTLE OL' ROCK TO ME.
WRITTEN BY
ART BALTAZAR & FRANCO
ARTWORK BY
SCOOT MCMAHON

HA!
IT'S NOT THE ROCK. IT'S THE CRYSTAL THAT'S IN THE ROCK!

SMACK!!

WITH THIS CRYSTAL IN MY POSSESSION, I WILL HAVE THE **ULTIMATE POWER** IN THE **UNIVERSE!**

IT DOESN'T BELONG TO YOU! IT BELONGS TO THE CRYSTAL CORPS!

FOOLISH PUP!
ONCE I ESCAPE THROUGH THAT SPACE PORTAL, I'LL BE UNSTOPPABLE!

SHEESH.
BAD GUYS ALWAYS TELLING GOOD GUYS THEIR PLANS!
CLICK!

SWOOSH!

KICK!
NO!
YOU MANGY MUTT!
THERE'S NO TELLING WHERE THE CRYSTAL IS HEADING!
IT'S LOST FOREVER!

—MIGHTY!

"ADVENTURE LIZARD!"
WRITTEN BY ART BALTAZAR AND FRANCO
ILLUSTRATED BY FRANCO
LETTERED BY MARSHALL DILLON
COLORED BY ARTHEE
UHHH...

OH NO, I'M A LIZARD!

HEY, LOOK AT THAT! I HAVE CAUDAL AUTOTOMY!

AHHHHHH! WHY DO I HAVE CAUDAL AUTOTOMY??!
WHY DO I KNOW WHAT THAT IS?

WHERE ARE MY ANTENNAE?
AND WHY DO I HAVE SCALES?

I'M HUNGRY.
I WONDER... WHAT DO LIZARDS EAT?
JUMP
CLICK
CLICK
BUGS? GROSS!
BUGS BUGS BUGS BUGS
ERK!
OH, LIZARDS CAN SHED THEIR SKIN?
RRRIIP!!
-APPEALING.

LATER...
ACTION CAT!
ARE YOU AWAKE?!
"the LIZARD WITHIN!"
PART 2

BUDDY! CAN YOU HEAR ME?

AAH! WHAT HAPPENED?!

YOU WERE BADLY ZAPPED BY EVIL CAT'S LIZARD GUN!

HOW BAD IS IT?

WHAT?!
YOU TRANSFORMED...
INTO...
INTO...
WELL...
WHAT?! WHAT?!

HOW DO I LOOK?

YOU LOOK LIKE A LIZARD.

HOW DO YOU FEEL?
I FEEL GREAT!

AND IT LOOKS LIKE I STILL HAVE MY SUPERPOWERS!
AW YEAH!

"LET'S USE OUR POWERS TO STOP THAT EVIL CAT!
"RIGHT NOW, HE'S LOOSE IN BEAUTIFUL DOWNTOWN SKOKIE!"
BBZZ!
BBZZ!
BBZZ!
HEH HA HA!

THE L-Z 5000 TRANSFORMATIONS HAVE BEGUN!

SOON, ALL THE CITIZENS OF SKOKIE WILL BE LIZARDS!

BBZZ!

BBZZ!

WELL, EVERYONE BUT THAT GUY!
eeee.

STOP RIGHT THERE, EVIL CAT!!
FINALLY!

SO, IF IT ISN'T...
ACTION CAAAAAAAHH!
WHAT HAPPENED TO YOU?!

OH MY GOSH, YOU LOOK AWFUL!
GREEN IS NOT YOUR COLOR!
A

HEY!

YOUR GIRLFRIEND, ON THE OTHER HAND...
SHE'S NOT MY--
YEAH, YEAH!
SHE WAS TOO FAST FOR MY LIZARD GUN!

UNTIL I FLIPPED THE SWITCH FROM LIZARD MODE...
CLICK!
LIZARD
BLIZZARD
...TO BLIZZARD MODE!

SHE'S FROZEN AND SITTING RIGHT OVER THERE!
HOW CONVENIENT, RIGHT?!
YOU FIEND!

NOW, ACTION LIZARD...
HEH, HEH...
...YOU WILL JOIN HER IN THE FROZEN TUNDRA!

TONGUE!

SLAP!
REVERSE
SWITCH!

BBZZZ!!

NO!
YOU TRICKED ME!
WITH YOUR...
DASTARDLY...
...LIZARD TONGUE OF TREACHERY!
I'M OUTTA HERE!
RUN
RUN
RUN
RUN
RUN

SWOOSH!
SPIN
SPIN
TWIRL
SPIN

AW MAN! C'MON!

MINUTES LATER...
THANKS FOR THAWING ME OUT, BOYS.
YOU'RE WELCOME.

SEE YOU NEXT TIME, ACTION.
POKE

?

ACTION CAT!
OH, NO!
NOT AGAIN!
SPEAK TO ME!
WHAT AN ADORABLE CAT!
NO!

-DONE!

LATER...
AW YEAH!
AW YEAH COMICS!
HEY, HAMMOND, WAIT TILL YOU HEAR THIS STORY...
"LIZARD BEAR!"
BY ART BALTAZAR & FRANCO & KURT WOOD
WRITERS
ARTIST

SO, UH... HEY, HAMMOND.
HI, GUYS.

DO YOU NOTICE ANYTHING DIFFERENT?
NOPE.
DID YOU GET A NEW SIGN?
NAH, I FOUND THE LIZARD GUN IN BACK AND...

...NEVER MIND.
SIP
SIP

WOW, HAMMOND! IS THAT A NEW VEST?

END!

CHAPTER TWO
REACTION CAT RETURNS!!
AND HE'S OVER-REACTING!
ART BALTAZAR ©2015

LATER THAT NIGHT,
IN BEAUTIFUL DOWNTOWN SKOKIE...
POUNCE!
LEAP!
JUMP!
I GET IT, A.C....
WE NEED OUR EXERCISE...

BUT WHY DO YOU CHOOSE THE MIDDLE OF THE NIGHT?
OH, THAT'S SIMPLE.

IT'S QUIET, IT'S CALM, AND THE SKYLINE LOOKS AWESOME.

PLUS, THE ENERGY IS LOW AND ALLOWS ME TO HEAR MY THOUGHTS.
AND WE GET TO SHOW OFF OUR NEW STEALTHY OUTFITS!

DANG! DANG!

SO MUCH FOR PEACE AND QUIET.

"OVER-REACTION CAT!"
DANG!
DANG!
DANG!
BY ART BALTAZAR & FRANCO
WRITER & ARTIST
WRITER
STORY PLOT BY MARC "BROTHER BEAR" HAMMOND

DANG! DANG!
I CAN'T TAKE IT ANYMORE!
BEING UP ALL NIGHT BY MYSELF IS SO...
...BORING!
BORING!
BORING!
BORING!

ACTION CAT?
NOT QUITE.

SIP!

I AM REACTION CAT!

WELL, YOU LOOK JUST LIKE ACTION CAT.
S

I AM NOT HIM!
I AM EVERYTHING OPPOSITE OF HIM!
S
OKAY.
CALM DOWN.

OPPOSITE LIKE...
...HE'S RED AND YELLOW...
...AND YOU'RE YELLOW AND RED?

THAT'S CORRECT!

WE'RE ALSO ON OPPOSITE SCHEDULES!
WHILE HE'S TUCKED IN HIS BED...

...I'M OUT HERE WANDERING AROUND ALL NIGHT!
WELL, THAT'S KIND OF OPPOSITE.

IT'S NOT! HE TRICKED ME!
HOW?

COFFEE IS NOT DOING IT ANYMORE.
I NEED SOMETHING STRONGER.

ALL-NIGHT
CONVENIENCE STORE
ENERGY
DRINKS
ON SALE
HERE!

ENERGY
DRINKS
ON SALE
HERE!
OF COURSE!
THAT'S IT!

GRAB!

PAY!

CHA-CHING!

I NEED TO STAY UP ALL NIGHT SO I CAN GET BACK TO DOING THE OPPOSITE OF ACTION CAT!

DRINK!
DRINK!
CHUG!

-TO BE CONTINUED!

"NIGHT-WALKING" STORY BY ART BALTAZAR AND FRANCO
ARTWORK BY FRANCO COLORS BY ARTHEE LETTERING BY MARSHALL DILLON

LATER,
IN THE EARLY MORNING...

ACTION
CAT!

WAKE UP,
HERO!
"OVER-
REACTION
CAT!"
Part 2
COME OUT
AND PLAAAY!

SSHH!
QUIET DOWN,
WILL YA?!

WHO'S
THAT?
IT LOOKS
LIKE...
...REACTION
CAT!

HOW SOON
YOU FORGET!
HOW DO YOU KNOW
WHERE WE LIVE?
I AM
YOU!
OH, RIGHT.

MONTHS AGO...
...I WAS CHASING DOWN THE NOTORIOUS EVIL CAT!
WHEN SUDDENLY, HE ZAPPED ME WITH THE EVIL-RAY 5000!
AARRGH!
ZAP!
SOMEHOW, GETTING ZAPPED BROUGHT OUT MY OPPOSITE SIDE!
REACTION CAT!
SO...

WHAT'S UP, R.C.?
YOU'RE LOOKING A BIT... MANGY.

IT'S STILL OPPOSITE OF YOU!

OKAY, OKAY. YOU DON'T HAVE TO OVERREACT!
THAT'S WHO I AM!

I'M OVER-REACTION CAT! I OVERREACT!

RIGHT, RIGHT.
YOU'RE AN OPPOSITE COPY OF ME.
SORT OF LIKE A CLONE?

I'M NO CLONE!
NOW, GET INTO COSTUME AND CHALLENGE ME!

OKAY, MAN!
THIS IS GETTING WEIRD!
PUSH!

YOU NEED TO CALM DOWN!
SHUT DOWN YOUR POWERS!

I CAN'T SHUT DOWN MY POWERS!
I DRANK ENERGY DRINKS TO STAY AWAKE!
NOW I'M OPPOSITE OF YOU!
HOW'S THAT OPPOSITE?
YOU NEED TO TAKE A NAP!

HERE, TRY SOME CHAMOMILE TEA!

NEVER!

I...
WILL...
STAY...
AWAKE...
UNTIL...

PING!
PING!
PING!
PING!
PING!
PING!

YARN
TRUCK

YARN
TRUCK
IT'S GONNA BLOW!
YARN

-TO BE CONCLUDED!

COFFEE
SHOP
COFFEE
"LOTS O'CREAM, LOTS O'SUGAR"
WRITTEN BY
ART BALTAZAR & FRANCO
ARTWORK BY
SCOOT MCMAHON

HAH!
FREE COFFEE!

SIP!
HEY!

STOP THAT THIEF!

HE OWES ME A DOLLAR FIFTY!
WE'LL CATCH HIM!

HE RAN THIS WAY!
AND HE WAS WEARING A GREEN VEST!

THERE HE IS!

AAH!

–NEXT TIME, TRY DECAF.

YOU ARE FINISHED, ACTION CAT!
FINISHED? I DIDN'T KNOW I STARTED!
"OVER-REACTION CAT!" Part 3
MY DIAMETRICALLY OPPOSED AGENDA HAS BEGUN!
YOU MEAN OPPOSITE?
THAT'S RIGHT!
I'M GONNA COVER THE CITY OF SKOKIE IN YARN!
MAKING IT HOT AND ITCHY AND DIFFICULT FOR CITIZENS TO WALK THEIR DOGS!
IT'S THE MIDDLE OF SUMMER...
...WHICH IS THE OPPOSITE OF WINTER!
HA!
YOU SEE WHAT I DID THERE?!
HUH?
THEN, I WILL TAKE OVER HARRISON, NEW YORK!
WHERE IS ADVENTURE BUG?
I NEED HIS HELP!

ELSEWHERE...
SO, WHAT BRINGS YOU TO THE MATTRESS EMPORIUM?
LOUIS
DON

I'M LOOKING TO BUY A WATERBED!

THIS ONE HERE IS A BEAUTY!
TOP OF THE LINE.

CAN I FILL IT WITH WARM MILK?
Y'KNOW, INSTEAD OF WATER?

UM...

...SURE. I SUPPOSE SO.

I'LL TAKE IT!

I AM OVER-REACTION CAT!
I WILL ALWAYS BE OPPOSITE OF YOU!
YOU TURN IT ON!
I TURN IT OFF!
YOU ARE SMOOTH, I AM FUZZY!
YOU FIX IT, I BREAK IT!
YOU READ BOOKS...
I SEE THE MOVIE!
OR SOMETIMES I LISTEN TO THE AUDIOBOOK!

YOU ARE TANGLED...

...AND I AM NOT!

YAH! YAH! LOUD!
AWAKE!
HA HA HEE HOH!
YARN! YARN!

SO HOW ABOUT THAT CHAMOMILE TEA?

GULP!

OH.
THAT WAS PRETTY GOOD.

mmmm...

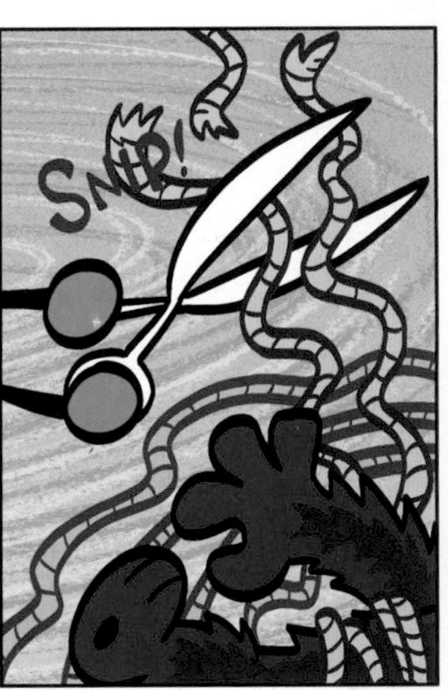

CATCH!
SLEEPY TIME, EVERY TIME.

—GOOD EVENING, SWEET DREAMS, AND GOOD AFTERNOON.

"MOON NAPPING"

by Artie and Franco and Kurt Wood!

CHAPTER THREE
AW YEAH! THIS IS BETTER THAN T.V.!
POP CORN
ART BALTAZAR 2015

AW YEAH DARK HORSE COMICS PRESENTS...

THE TOOTH WAS KNOCKED OUT DURING A FIGHT BETWEEN **ACTION CAT** AND **UNICORNEA**!

POW!

HOLY COW!

OH, YEAH.

I HEARD ABOUT THAT.

ENJOY.

SEE YA!
SWSSHH!!

AW YEAH!
WHAT A NICE ADDITION TO THE COLLECTION!

IT LOOKS GREAT!

WHO WAS AT THE DOOR?
IT WAS AWESOME BEAR.
HE GAVE ME A TOOTH.

THIS TOOTH?

I JUST PUT THE TOOTH ON THE SHELF!

HOW DID IT GET ON THE COUCH SO FAST?
SHAKE!
SHAKE!

GROWL! GROWL!

RARRG!
LOOK OUT! IT'S EVIL!
THE TOOTH HAS GONE WILD!

EAT!
HUNGRY!
BITE!
CHOMP!
BITE!
EAT!
HE'S QUITE HUNGRY!

LOOKS LIKE HE JUST WANTED SOME POPCORN!
SO MUCH FOR OUR T.V. SNACKS.

AW, THAT'S SWEET.
KISS!
LOOKS LIKE YOU HAVE A NEW GIRLFRIEND.

COOOO!
HE'S NOT MY GIRLFRIEND!

-AAWWW!!!

LATER...
READ
READ
DARK HORSE COMICS

MMM... SOMETHING SMELLS GOOD!
SNIFF! SNIFF!

HEY, ALOWICIOUS!
WHAT ARE YOU...

...COOKING?
HI, CORNELIUS!
SMELLS GREAT, HUH?

TOOTH-A-CORNEA IS BAKING CUPCAKES!
TOOTHA-WHAT?

YOU NAMED IT?
LOOKS LIKE WE MAY HAVE A SWEET TOOTH.
HOW ARE YOU DOING THIS, TOOTHA?
HOW ARE YOU FLOATING?

CAN I TRY?

YOUR DESSERTS LOOK DELICIOUS!

SMACK!

YOU MUST WAIT.
WHY?
THESE CUPCAKES ARE FOR CHAT-N-CHEW!

CHAT-N-CHEW! @ AW YEAH COMICS!
COOL.

LATER ... CHAT-N-CHEW @ AW YEAH COMICS!...
AW YEAH CHAT-N-CHEW!
THESE CUPCAKES ARE GREAT!
AW YEAH CONVERSATION!
GRRMM!

GREAT IDEA TO INVITE TOOTH-A-CORNEA AND HIS AWESOME BAKING SKILLS!

OUR CHAT-N-CHEW IS VERY SUCCESSFUL SINCE YOU BROUGHT THESE CAKES!

AW YEAH CAKES!!

YOU'D THINK A TOOTH FROM THE EVIL UNICORNEA WOULD BE EVIL!
BUT NOT THIS GUY!

HE IS THE MASTER OF ALL THINGS PASTRY!
BONUS!
ALL-AROUND NICE GUY!

THE CUPCAKES EVEN MADE NUCLEAR PLANT HAPPY!

GGRRMMM.

HA!
I GUESS WE HAVE A SWEET TOOTH AFTER ALL!

SMOOCH!

SOMETIMES A LITTLE TOO SWEET!

--SMITTEN.

"CLONE CAKES!"
MMMmm.
THE LAST ONE!
DELICIOUS!
AW YEAH TIME FOR SECONDS!

AND...THAT BITE MARK MATCHES THE BITE RADIUS OF THAT EVIL TOOTH!

ONLY ONE WAY TO FIND OUT WHO BIT THAT CAKE FOR SURE!
I WILL EXTRACT D.N.A.!

THEN, I SHALL USE THEIR JOY AGAINST THEM!
SWIPE!

HEY! ARE WE ALL OUT OF CAKE?
HA HA HEE HOH!

—CLONING!

MINUTES LATER...
...IN EVIL CAT'S UNDERGROUND SECRET LAIR...

I SHALL CREATE A SECRET ARMY OF EVIL CUPCAKES!
WE WILL CHEW UP THIS TOWN!
ACTION CAT WON'T KNOW WHAT BIT HIM!

ENOUGH PUNS!
THE CLONING PROCESS BEGINS!

BBZZZZZ

EVIL
EVIL
EVIL
EVIL
EVIL EVIL
HA! MY MINIONS!
EVIL
WE SHALL UNVEIL OUR EVIL DESSERTS UNTO THE WORLD!
NOW!
YOU WILL DO WHAT YOU DO SO NATURALLY!
EVIL
EVIL
EVIL
EVIL
KISS
KISS?
KISS
KISS
UH-OH! DOOMED BY SWEETNESS!

AND JUST LIKE THAT...
NNOOOO!!!
WHAT THE...?!
...A WICKED SCREAM IS HEARD THROUGHOUT THE TOWN OF SKOKIE!

OOOAAHRR!!!
CURSE YOU, AMAZING MOUSE!
SETTLE DOWN.

AAAAAA!

AARRGH!!
WHAT WAS THAT?!
I'M NOT SURE.

BUT I'LL TELL YA ONE THING, SHELLY...

...I WOULDN'T WANT TO BE ON THE RECEIVING END OF THAT SHRIEK OF SHRIEKINESS!
HA! ME NEITHER!
LIST
C'MON...
...LET'S GET THE NEXT ITEM ON OUR GROCERY LIST!

-GRAPE JUICE PLUS!

PFF!
PFF!
"AW YEAH HAUNTED GYM!"
STORY BY "AW YEAH HAAS" HASAN PASCHALL
ARTWORK BY ART BALTAZAR
PFF!
SO, SOUTHPAWS...

...DOESN'T WORKING OUT IN A HAUNTED GYM SCARE YOU?
NOPE!

BECAUSE... ONE DAY... I'M GONNA HAVE THAT BOXING REMATCH AGAINST ACTION CAT!

PUNCH!
PUNCH!

–I MUST BREAK YOU!

AAAHHH!!!

HELP!
CALM DOWN, BUDDY!
WHAT'S YOUR--

HAMMOND!
YA GOTTA HELP ME!
THEY'RE EVIL, I TELL YA!

THESE CAKES ARE EVERYWHERE!
IT'S TRUE!

I CAN'T HOLD 'EM!
THEY'RE LIKE ZOMBIES!

RARGH!
RARGH!
RARGH!
OKAY, SWEET CAKES...

...YOU NEED TO CALM DOWN!
MOVE ALONG.
NOTHING TO SEE HERE!

WAIT A MINUTE!
ARE YOU ACTION CAT?!
I AM!

HEY!
MY FELLOW CAKES!
IT'S THAT SUPERHERO WE READ ABOUT IN THE COMICS ON SUNDAYS!!

FOR REAL?!
WOW!
CAN WE HAVE YOUR AUTOGRAPH?!
WE'RE BIG FANS!
SUNDAYS?
WEREN'T YOU CAKES JUST CREATED A FEW MINUTES AGO?

SIGN MY COMIC!
OOH, I NEED YOUR AUTOGRAPH, TOO!
YOU'RE MY FAVORITE SUPERHERO!

DRAW ME A SKETCH!
ME, TOO!
ME, TOO!
ME, THREE!

SKETCH!
SKETCH!
AW YEAH COMICS

WHEW!
I'M SAFE!

WHAT?!
THEY LIKE HIM!
THOSE ARE MY MINIONS!

UM...PARDON ME, CUPCAKES...

YOU CAN'T HAVE A GREAT HERO WITHOUT AN EVEN GREATER VILLAIN!

HE'S RIGHT!
EVIL CAT IS THE REAL STAR!

HE LOOKS DELICIOUS!
MMM, TASTY!
I BET HE GOES GREAT WITH CATSUP!
WHAT?!

AAHH!!

WHERE'S EVIL CAT?
CHAT-N-CHEW IS ABOUT TO BEGIN!

HA!
JUST DESSERTS!
YOU KNOW IT!

-FIST BUMP!

LATER...
CLICK
CLICK

UM...
I'LL BE RIGHT BACK.
I'LL LEAVE YOU TWO ALONE.

CLICK
CLICK

STOMP!
STOMP!

LEAP!

FAREWELL, MY SWEET TOOTH.
BYE!

THAT REMINDS ME...
BOOM!
BOOM!
WALK!

...YOU HAVE A DENTIST APPOINTMENT TOMORROW.
BOOM!
BOOM!

—NO CAVITIES!

CHAPTER FOUR
ART BALTAZAR ©2015

SWIM
SWIM
SWIM

TREMOR
TREMOR

SHAKE
SHAKE

FFRREEEEEE!!
ACTION CAT
& ADVENTURE BUG
BY ART BALTAZAR & FRANCO
WRITER & ARTIST
WRITER

MEANWHILE, IN BEAUTIFUL DOWNTOWN SKOKIE...
AW YEAH COMICS!

G'MORNING, SEA CREECH!

FOOSH!

UH-OH.
SWOOSH!

ALOWICIOUS!
I THINK IT'S TIME TO GET INTO CHARACTER!
AW MAN!
SHE'S GLOWING AGAIN?
WHAT IS IT THIS TIME?

HELLO, BOYS.

PROBLEM WITH THE SEA CREECH AGAIN?
UM...
...WHAT DO YOU MEAN?
WHEW!
ALICE... I'M NOT FEELING SO GOOD.
SHELLY?

FOOSH!

FFOOSH!
DUCK!
HEADS UP!

UM...
...I GOTTA FINISH MY...
YEAH!
ME TOO!

SWOOSH!
SWOOP!
ZOOM!

TOO BAD WE HAD TO LEAVE ALICE SO QUICKLY.
NO WORRIES, PAL. I HAVE A FEELING WE'LL SEE HER AGAIN SOON.

OKAY... WHERE TO, BOYS?
SO, ANOTHER ALIEN INVASION?
SURE LOOKS THAT WAY!

OUR FRIENDS WENT THIS WAY?
THE OCEAN, AGAIN?
THEY TAKE US THERE EVERY TIME THEY START TO GLOW!

OH, NO!
IS THAT?
IT CAN'T BE!

MARQUAID LIVES!
WAIT A MINUTE...

...THAT'S MARQUAID?
HE LOOKS LIKE THAT GUY I SAW AT THE GROCERY STORE!

"AND I SAW HIM AT THE BUS STOP!

"AND AT THE POST OFFICE!
STAMPS
POST OFFIC

"AND AT THE MOVIE THEATER!

"AND IN THE PARK!

"AND DRINKING COFFEE THAT TIME!

"AND AT THAT COMIC SHOP IN BEAUTIFUL DOWNTOWN MUNCIE!"
AW YEAH COMICS!

I THINK THERE MAY BE A WHOLE BUNCH OF THESE GUYS!

WE ARE ONE!
WE ARE MARQUAID!

HELLO, SHELLY, MY DEAR.
HI, DAD.

DAD?!!

WHY... YES! IT'S TRUE!
SHELLY AND THE SEA CREECH ARE BOTH MY DAUGHTERS!
OBSERVE.
MY GIRLS ARE HERE TO ASSIST IN THE DESTRUCTION OF EARTH!

BUT... BUT... SHELLY... NEVER TOLD...
...AND THE SEA CREECH?
BAD NEWS, THAT ONE.

CALLING ALL MARQUAIDS!

MARQUAID!

MARQUAID!

MARQUAID!

MARQUAID!

MARQUAID!
MARQUAID!

BEHOLD, ACTION CATS!
THE MARQUAIDIANS HAVE ARRIVED!
AW NO!
AND YES!
THIS IS REALLY BAD FOR YOUR PLANET!

AND NOW...
...LITTLE KITTY...
...SINCE YOU ARE MY DAUGHTER'S BEST FRIEND...

...YOU CAN JOIN ME AS MY NEW APPRENTICE!
WHAT?!

NEVER!
YOU EVIL FIEND!

OH, SO DISAPPOINTING.
THAT'S TOO BAD.

DAD!
BLAST!
SO BE IT!

FFFFF
SPLASH!

NO!!
ADORABLE CAT!
DAD! SHE WAS MY BEST FRIEND!
THAT CAT IS JUST A MEASLY PEASANT STANDING IN THE WAY OF OUR WORLD DOMINATION!

I HAVE TO HELP HER!
PUNCH!
CURSE YOU, QUAID!
HA! YOU TICKLE ME!
FOOLS!
WHEN WILL YOU SEE YOU ARE ONLY A DISTRACTION?!

SPLASH!
PLEASE BE OKAY!

PLEASE BE OKAY!
PLEASE BE OKAY!

I'LL GIVE YOU SOME OF MY POWER!
PLEASE BE OKAY!

GRAB!
WHAT THE··?

HA!
NOW US MARQUAIDIANS WILL BECOME...
...ONE!

LET'S GO, BOYS!

HA HA HEE HOH!!

I THINK THIS IS REAL BAD, A.C.!
YEAH.

CONQUERED! WITH JUST A WAVE OF MY CLAW!

SPLOOSH!

THERE IS NO USE, FELLAS.
DON'T EVEN TRY.
MY FATHER WILL TAKE OVER THE WORLD.

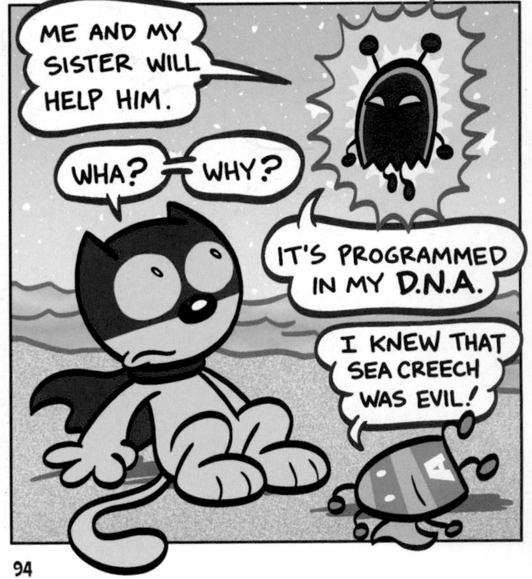
ME AND MY SISTER WILL HELP HIM.
WHA?
WHY?
IT'S PROGRAMMED IN MY D.N.A.
I KNEW THAT SEA CREECH WAS EVIL!

MY ADVICE IS TO STAY PUT.
STAY HERE ON THIS ISLAND!
STAY OUT OF MARQUAID'S WAY.
IT'S USELESS.

WE GOTTA TRY SOMETHING!

SWAT!

SPLASH!

UH-OH.

ACTION CAT!
ADORBS?
YES. IT'S ME.
GRAB MY HAND!
CAREFUL!
SHE'S WEARING GREEN AND PURPLE!

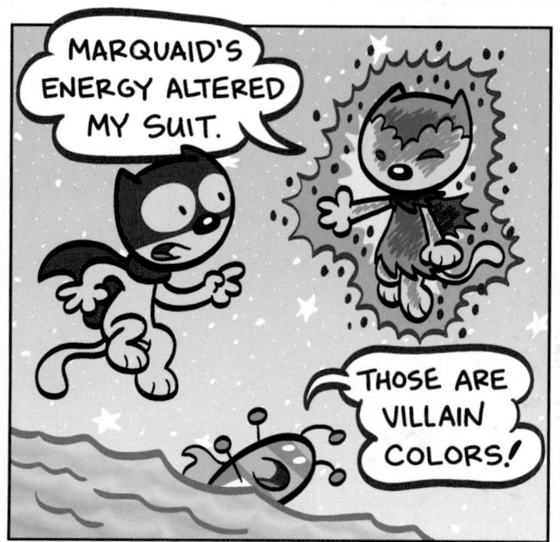
MARQUAID'S ENERGY ALTERED MY SUIT.
THOSE ARE VILLAIN COLORS!

RELAX. I'M NOT EVIL.

NOW, HANG ON!
WE'RE GETTING ALL CHARGED UP!

PUNCH!!

SHAKE
SHAKE
SHAKE
SHAKE
SHAKE
SHAKE

BOOOM!

CATCH!
CATCH!

TIME FOR YOU GUYS TO TAKE A TIME-OUT ON THIS ISLAND!
NO ONE WILL BOTHER YOU HERE!

SO... TELEKINESIS?
I DIDN'T KNOW YOU HAD THOSE POWERS.
NEITHER DID I!

SEA CREECH?

OFF SHE GOES.
INTO SPACE, IT LOOKS LIKE.
I'M SENSING A "SEARCH FOR THE SEA CREECH" SEQUEL.

EPILOGUE...
I TELL YA, ALOWICIOUS... THAT NEW ACTION CAT IS AWESOME YET STILL ADORABLE!
SURE. BUT NOT AS COOL AS THIS...

...HEY, WAITER!

ANOTHER LEMONADE REFILL, SIR?
YES, PLEASE.

POUR
POUR

CLINK!

AW YEAH, MAN!
THESE MARQUAIDIANS HAVE A GOOD THING GOING ON!
MARQUAID'S ISLAND RESORT
SAVING THE WORLD HAS NEVER BEEN SO REFRESHING!

—TRUE STORY.

★ SKETCHBOOK ★

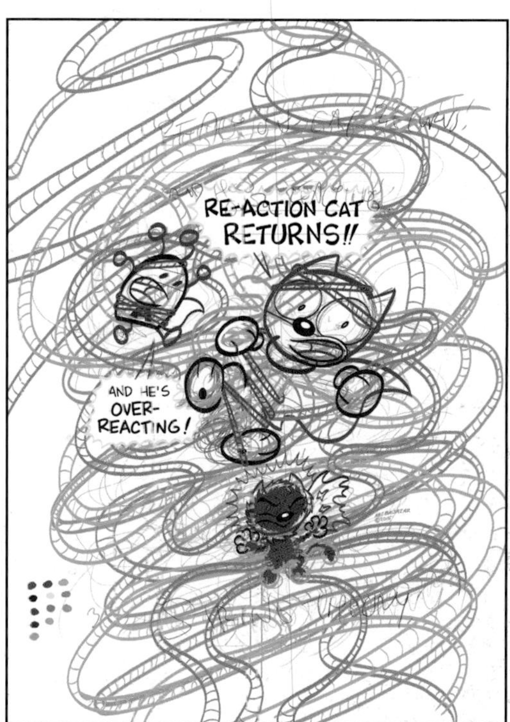

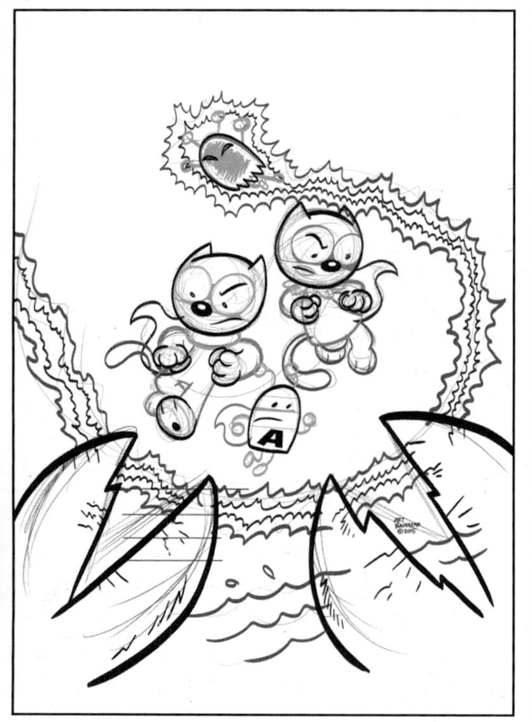

Cover sketches for Action Cat & Adventure Bug #1–#4

Rough layouts for "Over-Reaction Cat!"

ART BALTAZAR & FRANCO

THE CREATORS OF *TINY TITANS*, *SUPERMAN FAMILY ADVENTURES*, AND *AW YEAH COMICS!* COME TO DARK HORSE WITH A BIG BUNCH OF RIB-TICKLING, ALL-AGES BOOKS!

ITTY BITTY HELLBOY
978-1-61655-414-9 | $9.99

ITTY BITTY MASK
978-1-61655-683-9 | $12.99

AW YEAH COMICS! AND . . . ACTION!
978-1-61655-558-0 | $12.99

AW YEAH COMICS! TIME FOR . . . ADVENTURE!
978-1-61655-689-1 | $12.99

AW YEAH COMICS! MAKE WAY . . . FOR AWESOME!
978-1-50670-045-8 | $12.99

AW YEAH COMICS: ACTION CAT & ADVENTURE BUG
978-1-50670-023-6 | $12.99

GRIMMISS ISLAND
978-1-61655-768-3 | $12.99

ITTY BITTY HELLBOY: THE SEARCH FOR THE WERE-JAGUAR!
978-1-61655-801-7 | $12.99

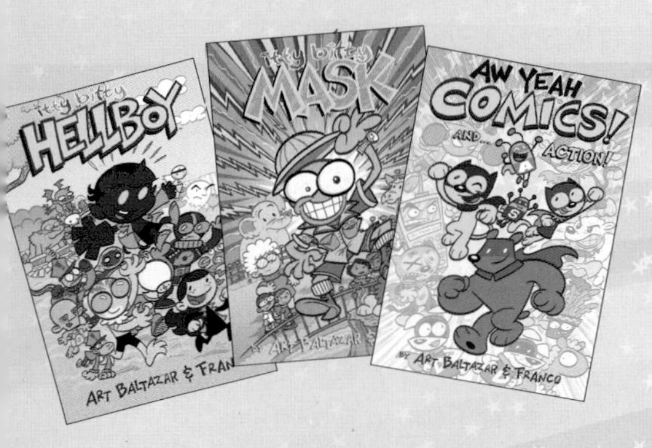

"Enjoyable work that fits quite nicely into hands of any age or in front of eyes of any child."
—Comic Book Resources

DarkHorse.com

AVAILABLE AT YOUR LOCAL COMICS SHOP OR BOOKSTORE
TO FIND A COMICS SHOP IN YOUR AREA, CALL 1-888-266-4226

For more information or to order direct: On the web: DarkHorse.com
Email: mailorder@darkhorse.com • Phone: 1-800-862-0052 Mon.–Fri. 9 AM to 5 PM Pacific Time.

DARK HORSE BOOKS

OTHER BOOKS FROM DARK HORSE

ITTY BITTY HELLBOY

Mike Mignola, Art Baltazar, Franco Aureliani

Witness the awesomeness that is *Hellboy*! The characters that sprung from Mike Mignola's imagination, with an AW YEAH Art Baltazar and Franco twist! This book has ALL the FUN, adventure, and AW YEAHNESS in one itty bitty package! That's a true story right there.

Volume 1: 978-1-61655-414-9 | $9.99
Volume 2: The Search for the Were-Jaguar! 978-1-61655-801-7 | $12.99

AVATAR: THE LAST AIRBENDER

Gene Luen Yang, Gurihiru

The wait is over! Ever since the conclusion of *Avatar: The Last Airbender*, its millions of fans have been hungry for more—and it's finally here! This series of digests rejoins Aang and friends for exciting new adventures, beginning with a face-off against the Fire Nation that threatens to throw the world into another war, testing all of Aang's powers and ingenuity!

THE PROMISE TPB
Book 1: 978-1-59582-811-8 | $10.99
Book 2: 978-1-59582-875-0 | $10.99
Book 3: 978-1-59582-941-2 | $10.99

THE SEARCH TPB
Book 1: 978-1-61655-054-7 | $10.99
Book 2: 978-1-61655-190-2 | $10.99
Book 3: 978-1-61655-184-1 | $10.99

THE RIFT TPB
Book 1: 978-1-61655-295-4 | $10.99
Book 2: 978-1-61655-296-1 | $10.99
Book 3: 978-1-61655-297-8 | $10.99

SMOKE AND SHADOW TPB
Book 1: 978-1-61655-761-4 | $10.99
Book 2: 978-1-61655-790-4 | $10.99
Book 3: 978-1-61655-838-3 | $10.99

THE PROMISE LIBRARY EDITION HC
978-1-61655-074-5 | $39.99

THE SEARCH LIBRARY EDITION HC
978-1-61655-226-8 | $39.99

THE RIFT LIBRARY EDITION HC
978-1-61655-550-4 | $39.99

PLANTS VS. ZOMBIES

Paul Tobin, Ron Chan

The confusing-yet-brilliant inventor known only as Crazy Dave helps his niece Patrice and young adventurer Nate Timely fend off Zomboss's latest attacks in this series of hilarious tales! Winner of over thirty Game of the Year awards, *Plants vs. Zombies* is now determined to shuffle onto all-ages bookshelves to tickle funny bones and thrill . . . *brains*.

LAWNMAGGEDON
978-1-61655-192-6 | $9.99

TIMEPOCALYPSE
978-1-61655-621-1 | $9.99

BULLY FOR YOU
978-1-61655-889-5 | $9.99

GARDEN WARFARE
978-1-61655-946-5 | $9.99

GROWN SWEET HOME
978-1-61655-971-7 | $9.99